What Kids Say About
Carole Marsh Mysteries . . .

I love the real locations! Reading the book always makes me want to go and visit them all on our next family vacation. My Mom says maybe, but I can't wait!

One day, I want to be a real kid in one of Ms. Marsh's mystery books. I think it would be fun, and I think I am a real character anyway. I filled out the application and sent it in and am keeping my fingers crossed!

History was not my favorite subject until I starting reading Carole Marsh Mysteries. Ms. Marsh really brings history to life. Also, she leaves room for the scary and fun.

I think Christina is so smart and brave. She is lucky to be in the mystery books because she gets to go to a lot of places. I always wonder just how much of the book is true and what is made up. Trying to figure that out is fun!

Grant is cool and funny! He makes me laugh a lot!!

I like that there are boys and girls in the story of different ages. Some mysteries I outgrow, but I can always find a favorite character to identify with in these books.

They are scary, but not too scary. They are funny. I learn a lot. There is always food, which makes me hungry. I feel like I am there.

What Parents and Teachers Say About Carole Marsh Mysteries . . .

"I think kids love these books because they have such a wealth of detail. I know I learn a lot reading them! It's an engaging way to look at the history of any place or event. I always say I'm only going to read one chapter to the kids, but that never happens—it's always two or three, at least!"
—Librarian

"Reading the mystery and going on the field trip—Scavenger Hunt in hand—was the most fun our class ever had! It really brought the place and its history to life. They loved the real kids characters and all the humor. I loved seeing them learn that reading is an experience to enjoy!"
—4th grade teacher

"Carole Marsh is really on to something with these unique mysteries. They are so clever; kids want to read them all. The Teacher's Guides are chock full of activities, recipes, and additional fascinating information. My kids thought I was an expert on the subject—and with this tool, I felt like it!"
—3rd grade teacher

"My students loved writing their own mystery book! Ms. Marsh's reproducible guidelines are a real jewel. They learned about copyright and ended up with their own book they were so proud of!"
—Reading/Writing Teacher

"The kids seem very realistic—my children seemed to relate to the characters. Also, it is educational by expanding their knowledge about the famous places in the books."

"They are what children like: mysteries and adventures with children they can relate to."

"Encourages reading for pleasure."

"This series is great. It can be used for reluctant readers, and as a history supplement."

MASTERS OF DISASTERS™

THE TREACHEROUS TORNADO MYSTERY

By
Carole Marsh

Managing Editor: Sherry Moss
Senior Editor: Janice Baker
Assistant Editor: Fran Kramer
Cover Design & Illustrations: John Kovaleski (www.kovaleski.com)
Content Design: Darryl Lilly, Outreach Graphics

Gallopade International is introducing SAT words that kids need to know
in each new book that we publish. The SAT words are bold in the story.
Look for this special logo beside each word in the glossary. Happy Learning!

yahoo.com is the property of Yahoo! Inc.

Gallopade is proud to be a member and supporter of these educational
organizations and associations:

American Booksellers Association

American Library Association

International Reading Association

National Association for Gifted Children

The National School Supply and Equipment Association

The National Council for the Social Studies

Museum Store Association

Association of Partners for Public Lands

A Note from the Author

As my family and I travel around the world in search of adventure and mystery, we often encounter more than we bargained for! Nasty weather is always a hazard. A tornado is certainly just about the "baddest" of bad weather!

When I was a little girl growing up in Atlanta, Georgia, I loved the story of Dorothy and her red, ruby slippers in the *Wizard of Oz*. But, boy howdy, that tornado business really scared me! I did not think we even had tornadoes in Georgia until one morning when my mom was taking my sister and me to school, she had to quickly pull the car into an auto repair garage. The sky had turned pea green and dime-size hail pelted the car windows. We felt safe until the wind began to whip so hard that it actually lifted our car off all four tires! Yep, a tornado was swirling outside!

I once saw a tornado form as a wispy, white cloud over a baseball field, causing everyone to scatter. I also watched a tornado form from picture-perfect, snow-white clouds in a bright-blue sky on an Iowa horizon. I've also seen waterspouts (tornadoes on water!) zigzag across the ocean!

But my favorite tornado story was when my own little girl, Michele, was four years old. We had a tornado watch, then a warning, near our home in Louisville, Kentucky. To keep her busy we said, "You just look out the window and tell us if you see anything." Suddenly, she said, "I see a BIG BLACK TRIANGLE!" In fear, we dashed to the basement and stayed a long time until the tornado was over. When we got back upstairs, the sun was shining. I asked my daughter, "What did you see?" She pointed out the window at the triangular shape of the roof peak next door—that was her "tornado!"

Good reading and good weather,

Carole Marsh

Hey, kids! As you see, here we are ready to embark on another of our exciting Carole Marsh Mystery adventures. My grandchildren often travel with me all over the world as I research new books. We have a great time together, and learn things we will carry with us for the rest of our lives!

I hope you will go to www.carolemarshmysteries.com and explore the many Carole Marsh Mysteries series!

Well, the *Mystery Girl* is all tuned up and ready for "take-off!" Gotta go...Papa says so! Wonder what I've forgotten this time?

Happy "Armchair Travel" Reading,
Mimi

ABOUT THE CHARACTERS

Artemis Masters is an absentminded genius. He's a scientist at the top of his field in the early detection of natural disasters. Everyone looks to him to solve the mysteries of nature…he just needs someone to find his car keys, shoes, and glasses!

Curie Masters, though only 12, has inherited her father's intelligence and ability to see things others don't. She has a natural penchant to solve mysteries…even if it means tangling with those older and supposedly smarter than her.

Nick Masters, an 8-year-old boy who's tall enough to pass as 12, likes to match wits with his sister and has her desire to solve mysteries others overlook. While he's the younger sibling, he tends to want to protect his sister and, of course, be the first to solve the mystery.

BOOKS IN THIS SERIES:

TABLE OF CONTENTS

CHAPTER ONE:

SOUNDING THE ALARM

"**Beep! Breeeep! Beep!**" screeched a little red box sitting in the Masters' living room.

"Head to the safe room!" yelled 11-year-old Curie Masters to her 8-year-old brother, Copernicus, nicknamed Nick, as she charged out of the house to a specially made safe room in the garage of their home.

The kids scrambled into the tiny space, and Curie secured the door.

"Wow, we did that in 15 seconds!" Nick said, breathless.

"But you forgot the cell phone!" Curie said. "And I didn't even think of turning off the gas and electricity like Dad showed us how to do in case the real thing happened! I forgot."

Nick, ever the optimist, answered, "Yeah, but it looks like Dad's Tornado Early Warning Device works—at least the alarm box 'beep, beep' part of it."

The two kids, hunched over on the concrete floor with their arms around their knees, looked up at the steel walls, reinforced door frame, and robust panel Curie had just bolted shut.

Nick, who was tall for his age—he looked almost 12—was feeling cramped, squished into the tiny room. "Curie, your elbow is poking my back," he complained.

"Well, whiffing your BO isn't exactly like smelling roses," Curie shot back. "Remember to bathe on the day a tornado hits, please!"

"Thanks, I'll keep that in mind," Nick replied, "If you have the sense not to wear that stinking perfume!"

The little room, no bigger than a large closet, was built by the kids and their scientist father, Artemis Masters, as a protection against tornadoes and other storms. The kids, named after Nicolaus Copernicus and Marie Curie, loved science—especially meteorology. They belonged to a network of kids interested in storm spotting, and had studied a great deal about tornadoes and all kinds of other storms. One project they had just completed was developing a Family Disaster Plan—what to do in case of severe environmental hazards. It included having a safe room in their home.

Curie, who liked to plan and organize things, had an idea. "While we are here," she said as she covered her nose, "let's go over the checklist of our emergency supplies, so we'll know if we are missing something."

"Here's the old list Dad helped us make," Nick said, pulling a piece of paper from the wall. "I'll read it. You see if we have everything."

"OK," Curie said, as she stood up to get a better look at

the boxes on the shelves above them—and distance her nose from Nick's smelly socks. She read from the list. "Canned food—yes, and we can't forget the can opener! Here it is on the shelf," she continued. "First aid kit, our vitamins, a bottle of Dad's blood pressure medication, and extra pairs of his glasses."

"How about a flashlight and radio, along with fresh batteries?" Nick asked. "I know we just bought those."

Curie said, "They're here, in the blue box, and our extra sets of clothes are in that big bag. We store the sleeping bags here anyway, and yesterday Dad brought in some bottled water—so I guess we can say we're prepared, if we don't count your baseball posters."

Nick was just about to respond to this wisecrack when a loud thump on the steel frame outside made the kids jump.

"Owww! My head!" a deep male voice bellowed.

Curie unbolted the door and yanked it open to see her father stumbling around, holding his head, a pair of glasses hanging from his neck while the pair that had been on his nose now lay in the path of his treading shoe.

"Stop! Don't move an inch!" Curie cried, too late, as a loud crunch sealed the fate of the doomed glasses.

"We have to paint that support beam yellow so I can see it!" Artemis said, as he lifted his foot up from the splintered lenses.

"It's a good thing we have extra glasses for these kinds of emergencies," Curie said jokingly, as she handed him a pair from the safe room. "We're just testing your design!"

"My design! You kids also helped, as I remember," Artemis said, "I probably wouldn't have built it if you hadn't insisted on making a safe room."

Nick and Curie had, indeed, urged their father to construct the little room in the garage. Of course, they participated in the design and construction. That spring, while other kids built tree houses, the Masters kids built a safe house.

It was a good thing the kids had learned so much about tornadoes, their Dad's beeping new invention, and protecting themselves. For very soon, the information would be needed!

CHAPTER TWO

SOUNDS OF DANGER

"Dad, your alarm gives a great beep!" Nick said.

"But it has one drawback," Curie added emphatically, eyeing her brother, "we found out that it doesn't allow enough time to shower before crowding into a small space with other people!"

"Well, it can't work miracles," Artemis said, teasing Nick for his habit of forgetting to shower daily. "But I hope it will save people's lives! That's why Dr. Brindle and I are working so hard on this gadget. We hope it will help people be better prepared for a tornado. Right

now, people don't have much advance warning other than by listening to the weather report."

"Why isn't just a weather report good enough?" Nick asked.

"Weather reports give information covering a large territory," Artemis replied. "The reports tell about regional weather patterns like huge cloud formations, but don't say what is happening in one little neighborhood."

A light went on in Nick's head. He said, "Your device will beep when a tornado touches down three streets away."

Curie added, "So this is a device people would want to buy and put in their homes."

"You got it!" Artemis said, proud of his kids. "You both are chips off the old block."

Artemis was a smart, but sometimes absent-minded, scientist who studied seismic events such as earthquakes. His Earthquake Early Warning Device monitored sounds the ground makes before and during the event. By learning about these sounds, he hoped it might be possible to predict when an earthquake would strike. This would allow people to get to a safe area quickly.

Artemis was gaining some success in this field of study, making him well-known to other scientists. That is why an expert in tornadoes, Radnor Brindle, asked for Artemis' help in developing something similar for predicting tornadoes.

"Can the beeper actually hear when a tornado touches down?" Nick asked, almost not believing such a thing could be possible.

"The beeper is just ears and a voice, with a small brain," Artemis replied. "When it hears a special signal from the big brain computer, it sets off the beep. The computer does the difficult work. It has to sort all the sounds it hears from sensors placed in the ground."

"A sensor hears all the noises in the area?" Nick asked.

"Just about," his father said. "The sensor records and

transmits all sorts of sounds, like trucks driving by and cows grazing in the fields. The computer hears the sounds from the sensors and knows when it's hearing a tornado touching down on the ground. When that happens, it sends a message to the beeper, setting off the alarm."

Nick look puzzled. "Does a tornado make a special sound?"

"Studies have shown that the tornado **vortex** itself has a sound," Artemis explained. "Then there may be a sound it makes when it touches down, causing debris to fly around. We call the screen image that is created from the sound waves, or light waves in some cases, a tornado's 'signature.' Dr. Brindle is helping me code the computer to recognize the sound waves and create the signatures—just like you can recognize my signature by my handwriting."

"Is Dr. Brindle coming over to the house today?" Curie asked hopefully. She was fond of Dr. Brindle. He was like their father in that he could be very childlike and funloving, but he was the opposite in appearance. Where Artemis was tall and thin with wild, spiky hair, Dr. Brindle was short and round and had no hair, even on his eyebrows. His thick, black-rimmed glasses made up for the lack of eyebrows in defining his eyes.

"I expect he will," said Artemis. "I need to get his new code. It's supposed to tell the computer when a tornado has landed, letting us know the sounds of danger. It is the critical piece of the Tornado Early Warning Device."

"I hope he'll come!" Curie exclaimed. "He's the only adult I know over 35 who wants to learn how to text message! Even you don't know how to do that!"

"Curie, my fingers are way too slow and clumsy," said Artemis. "Besides, I would much rather talk to somebody over the phone than send them a text message. Hearing the person's voice on the line tells me a lot about how that person is feeling."

"Dad, text messaging has emoticons," Curie said, as she keystroked in the famous round face with a smile, ☺, on her cell phone. She showed the display to her father. "You just plug in one little icon that symbolizes your feeling in your message and the person gets the message. Everyone knows that this smiley face shows you are happy."

She added, "Here is a kiss, Dad," as she typed the key strokes :-* on her cell phone keypad to show her father.

"I'd rather get a real kiss!" Artemis said, laughing.

Curie shook her head. Even though Curie was very bright, sometimes it was beyond her to understand the ways of the older generation.

"You just don't have the patience to learn, Dad," teased Nick. "It's like learning a new language."

"I already know five spoken languages and several computing languages," Artemis said. "I don't need to learn another language at my age! You can keep teaching Dr. Brindle to text message. He loves it."

"Now, where were we before I set off the alarm?" Artemis asked, as he absentmindedly put the glasses hanging around his neck right next to the ones already on his nose!

"We were getting the van ready for the trip," Curie reminded her father. "And if you can't see, it's because you really only need one pair of glasses!"

"Oh yes, oh yes," Artemis said, blinking as he pulled off the extra glasses. "Ah, that's better." With his visual field clear, he could somehow think more clearly, and began giving instructions. "Now, for the trip to Tornado Alley—Nick, come help me pack the Tornado Early

Warning Device, the computer, and the sensors in the van. Curie, make sure my papers over there are put in the file box. You know the filing system."

Curie sighed as she saw the mountains of papers strewn about the room as if a tornado had hit them. Filing papers—what a way to spend a summer vacation! Curie sincerely hoped the trip to Tornado Alley would be more exciting. Dad promised it would be.

Because of their storm-spotting knowledge and problem-solving abilities, Artemis was taking his kids on a storm-chasing adventure to test his new device. They would plant the devices in the ground just before a tornado warning was issued for that area. Artemis would run the program and hope for the best when he heard the beeper go off. The kids would bring their own laptops and cell phones to assist in data entry and communications. Artemis thought it would be a great "internship" for both of the kids, who wanted to become scientists someday.

The van was soon packed, and it was time to depart. The kids called friends and family members to say goodbye. They also checked e-mails from their friends. Nick saw one odd message from an e-mail address he didn't recognize. The subject line read "☺ cuz taken." He was always getting weird spam like that so he didn't open it up, or give it much thought.

Radnor Brindle still had not contacted them. Artemis tried reaching Radnor on the phone several times. Finally, he hung up the receiver in frustration and groaned, "Where is Radnor when I really need him? All I hear is a ringing phone. This is not like him to be unreachable."

"Are we going to wait for him?" Curie asked, worried about Dr. Brindle.

"I told him we have to leave by a certain time," Artemis replied. "That time is now. Let's try calling him from our cell phones later.

He knows my cell phone number. He can always call me. And he can always e-mail us the code."

Was Radnor's ringing phone, like the alarm box, another sound of danger? Were there other strange things happening they didn't see?

CHAPTER THREE:

YOU MIGHT AS WELL CHASE THE WIND

Nick, wedged in the back seat amid the supply boxes and computers, waited for the family ritual marking the start of an adventurous road trip. Right on cue, Artemis said, "Pilot to co-pilot. All systems go?"

Then Curie, sitting in the passenger seat up front, replied, "Roger that, captain. All systems are A-OK. Kick the tires and light the fires!"

Artemis hit the accelerator and the van rolled out of the driveway, on the road to a new adventure.

"Are we going to Oklahoma first?" Nick asked.

"Yep, that's the plan," said Artemis. "There's a good chance of finding tornadoes there. It will be a long ride, though. Sit back and enjoy the scenery."

On the long trip to Oklahoma, the kids amused themselves by talking about tornadoes, a subject that never bored them.

"A kid in my class thought that Tornado Alley was a street name," Nick said. "So I told him it was an area covering many states including Oklahoma, Texas, Kansas, and Nebraska. It's called Tornado Alley because most of the tornadoes in the United States strike in this area."

"Dad, which state gets hit the worst with big tornadoes?" Curie asked.

Artemis answered, "Texas—maybe because it's the biggest state in the lower 48 states."

"What was the worst tornado to hit the United States?" Nick asked his father.

He was fascinated by the power of really big tornadoes.

"Well, that depends on what you mean by 'worst,'" Artemis said. "The worst in terms of size and scope and total number of people killed was the Tri-State Tornado that struck on March 18, 1925. It killed 695 people in Missouri, Illinois, and Indiana as it traveled about 219 miles! That was an F-5, the most powerful on the F-Scale. Do you know what the F-Scale is?"

"Oh, yeah," Nick said, "That's the way scientists estimate the wind speed of a tornado by the type of damage it caused. For example, an F-0, the weakest tornado, blows only about 70 miles an hour or less because there's just light damage like broken tree branches. F-1's blow about 100 miles per hour, enough to peel off pieces of roof. F-3's actually tear the roof off at 150 mph. So an F-5 is a total disaster!"

"Yes, powerful tornadoes are terrible, especially in highly

populated areas," Artemis agreed. "The Worcester, Massachusetts Tornado in 1953 has the record for the most number of people killed in a limited area—about 90 people. More than one thousand people were injured. The tornado was so powerful that pieces of mattresses were lifted up into the clouds, coated with ice, and dropped into Boston Harbor nearly 45 miles away!"

"Massachusetts—that's not anywhere near Tornado Alley!" Curie said.

Artemis agreed. "That's right. Bad tornadoes can happen anywhere, except maybe Antarctica."

"Nick," Curie asked, "didn't you write a report about a tornado that struck at a really strange time—almost magical?"

"Oh yeah, the Tornado of the Elevens," Nick said. "It struck in Michigan at 11:11 P.M. on 11/11/11! Isn't that creepy?"

It seemed like they had been traveling forever when Nick said, "Dad, look at that sign—Oklahoma Welcomes You. We're here! Now what?"

"We may be in Oklahoma alright, but now we just need to find a fine tornado!" Artemis replied.

"There isn't much here except flat ground and sky," Nick replied. "It shouldn't be hard to find anything—even for Dad without his glasses."

Artemis turned on the car radio to listen to weather reports.

He scanned all the available radio stations and listened to the forecasts. The weathermen were predicting clear skies and relatively cool air. The chance of tornadoes was way down.

Curie, who was getting bored and sore from sitting so long said, "Dad, did we come all this way for nothing?"

Oklahoma Welcomes You

Artemis, who knew how quickly weather can change, answered with an old saying, "If you don't like the weather, wait a moment. We'll just have to wait. Let's check into a motel and see if we can get hold of Dr. Brindle."

In the motel room, Curie set up her laptop. She glanced over the long list of e-mails from her friends. There was nothing from Dr. Brindle. She checked her cell phone. Again, there were plenty of messages from friends but no messages from "MisterTwister," Dr. Brindle's screen name.

Artemis checked his e-mail. He even tried phoning. "Still no word of Radnor," he said, even more concerned than before. "What could've happened to him? He knows I need that code. If we had it, we could be operational tomorrow when we go storm chasing."

It was worrisome and frustrating. Also, the weather was not cooperating—there were clear skies, cool air, and no frontal system blowing east—when what they needed was a good old-fashioned thunderstorm.

The next day proved to be the same— no news of thunderstorms in the immediate area and no word from Radnor. Artemis was worried. "We're wasting precious time just sitting here," he said. "I don't want to drive all over the place without a good chance of meeting a thunderstorm. I guess tomorrow we'll have to chase the wind in Kansas!"

Be careful what you ask for...

CHAPTER FOUR:

DUST DEVILS

Artemis and the kids listened to the various regional weather reports. Just as Artemis had thought, some thunderstorms could be brewing in southern Kansas the next day. They made the van ready for an early departure the next morning.

Feeling confined in the motel room, Curie and Nick decided to take a dip in the motel swimming pool. After a quick swim, they stretched out on their towels to catch the last rays of the sun.

"Hey Nick, check out those two vans over there," Curie said, as she eyed the motel parking lot. "They must be storm chasers like us, looking for a big tornado."

The two vans were parked near, but not next to, each other. One van was bright red with the words *Tornado Chaser* written in gigantic letters across the side panel. Below the lettering, there was a picture of a cowboy sticking his head out the window of a van, madly pursuing the gray funnel of a tornado.

"What weird dudes," Nick said, as he saw some lanky, scraggily-haired young men unpacking gear and a motorcycle from *Tornado Chaser*. They were dressed in muddy jeans, dust-covered red T-shirts, and grungy cowboy hats. After unpacking, the guys lazily tossed around a Frisbee in the parking lot.

"They look like they haven't slept, showered, or shaved in a week! In their dirty red shirts, they look like dust devils," Curie added, referring to the little, dancing whirlwinds of dirt and dust that blow on a hot, clear day.

"The guys in the other van sure look different," Curie added, as she checked out the two clean-cut young men wearing polo shirts, khaki pants, and loafers who were also unloading their gear. The two men did not

stick around, but quickly disappeared into a motel room. The rear section of their van had no windows, but only the expression *Twister Teaser* painted boldly in blue across a white background. The sides of the van displayed a few painted blue lines meant to depict an **abstract** image of tornadoes.

As the kids watched the storm chasers, still another huge van, more like a small bus, arrived. It was gaudily painted in bright yellow, sporting huge red lettering spelling out *Tornado Thrills, Inc.* on the sides. As soon as it stopped, passengers of all ages emerged, stretched their legs, and lugged their bags to the motel office.

"Grannies with straw hats, old men in baseball caps carrying binoculars, moms with kids littler than us!" Nick exclaimed. "Those people can't be real storm chasers! They look like sightseers on a trip to the Grand Canyon!"

"I heard that tourists will pay money to see a real tornado, like people who pay to go whale watching," Curie answered. "I hope the tour guide is careful."

As the sun dropped behind the horizon, the kids returned to their motel room to change. They told their father about the three storm chaser vans in the parking lot and then checked their e-mail.

"Hey, I got an e-mail from MisterTwister!" Curie yelled, as she scanned the list of e-mail screen names.

"What does Dr. Brindle say?" Artemis asked. "I tried calling him again when you went swimming but still got no answer."

"He says he has decided to do his own storm chasing, and not to worry about him," Curie said. "But he doesn't say where he's going."

"Does he say anything about the code and when I will get it?" Artemis asked.

"He just says it needs more testing," Curie replied.

"Now, that is really weird..." Artemis said. "I can't believe he's run off chasing his own storms. We decided that I would do this part of the project because he hates traveling."

"He's such a homebody who loves gourmet food," Curie agreed. "I can't imagine Dr. Brindle driving all over the country eating fast food and sleeping in strange beds while trying to chase a tornado."

"Curie, you are right about Radnor," Artemis said. "This isn't like him to tell me now that the code needs more testing. He said the code was ready. He's usually very responsible. I don't like the sound of this."

Curie added, "There's something strange about this e-mail. The words he uses just don't sound like the way he usually writes to me. The expressions are too formal. He usually makes me laugh when he writes words my friends and I use like 'dude' and 'awesome.'"

"Yeah," said Nick. "Dr. Brindle used to send me e-mails, too. They didn't sound like this one!"

Curie thought this strange e-mail could possibly be a clue to what happened to Dr. Brindle. Was he trying to tell her something?

CHAPTER FIVE:

QUESTIONS AND CLUES, PLEASE

The next day, Artemis and the kids set out in the van for Kansas where the weather forecasters were promising some serious thunderstorms.

As usual, after hearing the latest weather reports, the topic of tornadoes quickly came up.

"Dad, what really causes a tornado?" Nick asked. "And why do so many tornadoes hit Tornado Alley?"

"Let me answer that one, Dad," Curie piped up. "I know the answer!"

"OK," Artemis said, "You give it a try."

Curie began, "Those are really good questions, Nick. Scientists still don't know much about what actually causes the spin of a tornado. They think that the warm, moist air, because it is lighter than the cold air above it, moves upward. The rising warm air meets other winds moving around it—like the warm air being a pencil between the palms of your hands, and your hands being winds moving in opposite directions. The pencil will rotate."

"You gave a **concise** answer!" Artemis said, "Short and to the point."

"And why Tornado Alley, Dad?" Nick asked, preferring his father to answer his question. He didn't like being outsmarted by his sister, and often competed against her in the rough and tumble of everyday life. However, their closeness prevented a real **antagonism** from forming.

"The turbulent wind and temperature conditions in Tornado Alley make it a perfect place for tornadoes to form," Artemis explained. "Tornado Alley is a great flatland corridor between the Appalachian Mountains in the east and the Rocky Mountains in the west. Cold air is pushed south from Canada. Hot air is pushed north from Mexico and the

Gulf of Mexico. The two frontal boundaries collide in Tornado Alley because they have nowhere else to go."

"Setting up the conditions for a tornado," Curie noted, showing off her knowledge to Nick.

"When the conditions are right," Artemis continued, "tornadoes can occur anytime. But they do have their seasons. In the southern part of Tornado Alley, twisters occur more often in late winter and early spring. In the northern part, they mostly occur in late summer."

"Nick," Curie asked, testing her brother, "Do you know the average size of a tornado?"

"Yeah, that's easy!" Nick answered, glad to now show off his knowledge. "The average size is 500 feet across. But they come in all sizes. Some funnels are long and thin. Some are short and wide. And they come in different colors—like your cell phone."

"Different colors?" asked Curie. She hadn't heard of this before.

"Yeah," Nick continued, glad to know something she didn't. "Tornadoes are basically invisible because they're just air blowing around. But depending on what is blowing in them, they can be different colors. For example, if the dirt they suck up is red, they'll be reddish. If they travel over water, they can turn white or blue."

Artemis added, "Remember that tornadoes may not have a color, basically making them invisible. Sometimes you just can't see a tornado, like at night when it's dark. I've heard stories where people never saw anything but heard a loud roar that sounded like a train going by. Those kinds of twisters are particularly dangerous."

"In those cases, your warning device would really be helpful in saving lives," Nick commented.

"Yes, indeed," Artemis said. "Whenever you can't see much, such as at night or during an invisible tornado, this little device will make noise when a tornado is out there."

Nick, now feeling confident in his knowledge, challenged his sister, "I bet I know something you don't!"

"What?" Curie said, "Betchya don't! Try me."

"Do tornadoes rotate clockwise or counterclockwise?" Nick asked, grinning.

Curie wrinkled her nose. Had her little brother beaten her?

"I'll give you a clue," Artemis said. "They rotate like hurricanes."

"Oh, then I know," Curie beamed. "In the northern hemisphere, tornadoes would blow counterclockwise. And in the southern hemisphere, they would blow clockwise."

"An 'A' to you," Artemis said, smiling.

"No fair, Dad," Nick challenged. "You gave her a clue. She always figures things out from clues."

Artemis changed the subject abruptly. "Curie," he said, "you should start looking for clues to what happened to Dr. Brindle. We need him."

Curie wished she could figure out where Dr. Brindle was and why he had sent the strange e-mail. She needed more clues! After all, there was a dark cloud on the horizon!

CHAPTER SIX:

YES, TOTO, IT REALLY IS KANSAS!

"Look at that sign, Dad!" Curie yelled. "I think we're in Kansas!"

Artemis laughed, and said, "Yes, Toto, it really is Kansas!"

"Oh, Dad," Curie said, as she rolled her eyes. Dad's humor was so weird!

They soon reached the designated spot for putting down the listening devices where weather reports suggested thunderstorms would appear later that day.

Artemis, Curie, and Nick quickly unloaded the equipment from the van. Artemis showed the

Kansas Welcomes You

kids how to activate and bury the listening devices a foot or so underground.

"How do we find them when we want to dig them up?" Nick asked. "We can't put up a flag to mark them. That would blow away in a tornado."

"I have a handheld device that picks up their signal," Artemis said. "It also has a Global Positioning Program. With those aids, the monitor will display the locations."

As she packed the earth down around a sensor, Curie asked, "Are these sensors useful if we don't have Dr. Brindle's code?"

Artemis stood up with a grim look on his face. "Maybe we can at least collect data if we can't interpret it," he said. "We can test the collection process."

After burying their devices, Artemis and the kids got back in the van. All they could do now was wait. Artemis turned on the radio. He soon broke into a wide grin. Three weather reports said that yes, a tornado watch was on for the local area!

Artemis asked one last question as he started the van. "OK, kids, do you know the difference between a tornado watch and a tornado warning?"

Curie spoke first. "I do!" she shouted. "A tornado *watch* means there's a strong likelihood a tornado could strike. The conditions are present and people should watch out and listen to weather reports. A tornado *warning* is more serious. It means that a tornado has been seen or shown by radar. Everyone should act to protect themselves and their pets, like by going to a shelter."

As Curie spoke, the sky darkened rapidly. Heavy gray clouds formed on the distant horizon, moving their way. The air suddenly became very still. It was getting scary!

Nick said solemnly, "I guess it might be Tornado Time!"

CHAPTER SEVEN:

SIGNS OF DANGER

Curie tried to remember what they had learned about tornado preparedness. To break the eerie silence in the van, she said, "Well, we're doing the right things. We're listening to the radio for the latest weather reports. We're watching the approaching storm. Now we need to look for the danger signs."

"What are those?" Nick asked, not sure that he really wanted to know. What would they do if they saw the danger signs? He suddenly realized they didn't have a shelter to go to!

"Look for dark, almost greenish skies," Curie said, "and a low-hanging dark cloud, especially one that might be rotating."

"None of those signs are out there now," Nick said, as he peered out at the dark horizon, almost hoping nothing like that would appear. Now that he was actually at a spot where a tornado could strike, he wasn't sure he wanted to see it!

Curie continued reciting the danger signs. "Other signs are large pieces of hail, and a loud roar, like the sound of a freight train."

"None of those, either," Nick said, letting out a sigh of relief.

By the time Curie finished her watch list, the wind had kicked up dust everywhere.

Nick asked, "Dad, what are we supposed to do if we see a tornado and don't have a shelter to go to? Like now?"

"Good question," Artemis said. "If the tornado is far away or moving away, drive as fast as the speed limit will allow, evacuating the area. That's what we plan to do, as soon as I start the computer program."

"Dad, what if the tornado forms close to us or if we can't drive away?" Nick asked.

"In that case," Artemis said, "we have to get out of the van and high-tail it to a ditch. What's the expression I taught you?"

"Go low, get low!" Nick piped up.

"You bet!" Artemis said. "You get as low as you can and hug the ground for all you're worth!"

A torrential downpour suddenly broke out—as if enormous buckets of water were being dumped from the heavens. Soon, the rain was so fierce that they could hardly see the road ahead or behind them—much less the horizon in the distance. Nick and Curie were glad their dad parked on the side of the road. Imagine trying to drive in this!

Suddenly, they heard loud "**clack, clack**" sounds.

"Hail," Artemis said, as he saw the ice pellets whack the windshield.

Curie felt every nerve in her body tingle with excitement. The hail was almost as big as marbles. What if the windshield shattered? She asked her father, "Isn't this one of the dangerous conditions that accompanies a tornado?"

"Yes, Curie," Artemis said. "We also need to watch for lightning. . ."

At that very moment, a bolt of lightning, as if summoned by Artemis' magical voice, lit up the sky.

Everyone laughed. It eased the tension.

"Dad, you're a wizard!" Nick said.

"Like I said," Artemis continued, "lightning and flash floods. I have to be careful that we don't drive through some gulley where our van could be washed away!"

"We can't forget the straight-moving wind around a tornado," Curie said. "It can also blow very fast in a thunderstorm."

The hail eased up a bit, but the rain was growing more torrential. In the murky downpour, the kids looked for the funnel of a tornado.

"See anything, kids?" Artemis asked as he readied his laptop computer.

"I see something, but it's not a tornado. Dad, I think we have company," Curie said. "Look behind us."

Through the pouring rain, two sets of blurry headlights could be seen approaching. One set of headlights stopped moving, and shortly afterward the second pair stopped.

They were somewhere in a Kansas corn field, which seemed like the end of the world to Curie and Nick.

Who else could be out here? Were they being followed? Was this another sign of danger?

CHAPTER EIGHT:

NOTHING BUT HOT AIR!

In the back seat, the kids continued to scan the horizon for a tornado, ready to help in any way they could. While their eyes were glued on the skies, their ears were tuned to the van radio, still blaring reports of the tornado watch.

The wind and rain pummeled the van, making it rock and shake. Nick could only imagine a big giant playing with their van like he would play with a toy truck. The rocking was so fierce, Artemis' glasses slid off his nose and his laptop computer slipped from the seat to the floor.

"Dad, your laptop needs a seat belt!" Nick exclaimed.

"Thank goodness my glasses are on a chain around my neck," Artemis said, as he put his glasses back on and buckled up the laptop in the seat next to him. Then he powered up the laptop to run the data collection program.

The computer program sprang to life with bells and whistles. Instead of, *You've got mail,* Dr. Brindle had programmed his software to say, *You've got the conditions for a tornado! Kick the tires and light the fires!*

"That crazy Radnor!" Artemis said, as he and the kids burst out laughing.

Artemis hit the command keys to start the data input. The laptop hummed efficiently as it received a steady stream of information.

"It looks like the data collection software is working!" Artemis shouted. "Data appears to be coming from the listening devices we planted in the ground!"

Just as the software kicked in, the heavy downpour abruptly stopped. The clouds thinned and disappeared. A sudden stillness hung in the air. The only noises were the *drip, drip, drip* of rainwater falling off the van, and the click of the laptop keys as Artemis shut down his computer program.

"Oh, rats!" griped Curie. The sun peeking out of the clouds put a damper on their project.

"Looks like our tornado got rained out," Nick said. "Do we get a rain check, Dad?"

Artemis, trying not to show his disappointment, said, "Well, it gives us more time to get the code from Dr. Brindle. Next time, maybe we'll have the code and can run the whole program—not just the data collection part."

With the clearing skies, the kids could easily see more than the headlights of the other vehicles parked nearby. The two vans were the same ones they had seen at the motel—they had the markings *Twister Teaser* and *Tornado Chaser* on them.

"They must have heard the radio reports, too," Curie remarked.

The dust-covered young men in *Tornado Chaser* climbed out of their van. They stretched their legs by walking around their vehicle. They teased and shouted to each other as they gulped down water and sodas.

The other van, *Twister Teaser,* was parked a little further away. Its occupants, the two clean-cut young men, were also stretching their legs. They didn't say much to each other but looked silently at the landscape and the vans nearby. Then they climbed back inside their van.

Artemis and the kids decided to take a stretch, too. Curie dug out some apples from a sack in the back seat and passed one to Artemis and one to Nick. As they munched on the fruit, she noticed her father was quieter than usual.

"Dad, you look worried," she said.

"I am. There are too many strange things going on," Artemis said.

Curie was about to suggest that she and Nick go into the fields to dig up the sensors. She eyed the other vans, and thought it might be better to hold off doing that. An awful idea had popped into her head. "Dad, do you think someone else could collect our data? I mean, if we can collect data here from the boxes we buried, surely somebody else can, too. You don't have any security built into this prototype, do you?"

"Since this was just a test model," Artemis said, "we didn't feel the need to build in a security layer. You're right. Someone else could collect our data if they are near the sensors we buried."

"Like the guys in those two vans?" she asked.

"Yeah, like them," Artemis snapped. He was angry.

Curie knew her father's early warning device could be of great value. Other people might want to get hold of it, or the code—or worse, get hold of Radnor, or her father. She was suddenly afraid.

Were her fears, like the storm that had just passed, nothing but hot air?

CHAPTER NINE:

GRAND CENTRAL STATION IN KANSAS

"Oh my gosh, Dad!" Curie yelled. "Look what's coming! It's the third van with all the tourists—the *Tornado Thrills, Inc.* tour group we told you about!"

Artemis turned to see the large, garish yellow van pull up near the Masters' van. The passengers looked like a flock of cackling geese getting off the bus. He frowned and said, "Another van! This place is getting to be more and more like Grand Central Station. It wouldn't surprise me if Radnor himself suddenly showed up!"

Curie had to smile when she pictured Grand Central Station in New York City. Last summer, she was there with her family. The image that came to her mind was of 10,000 people of every conceivable size and shape coming and going in that massive train station.

"Let's wait until these vans leave before we retrieve the listening devices," Artemis suggested. "We don't need the world to know what we are doing here. Let them think I'm just a crazy dad taking his kids on a wild adventure."

"But you are," Nick muttered under his breath. He saw some of the guys from *Tornado Chaser* head their way, and said, "Dad, let's hide the equipment under a blanket so they won't see it!"

"Good idea, Nick," Curie said, as she pushed some scientific reports under the seat. She put a big bag of potato chips on top of a box of sensors.

The two tall guys in the red T-shirts swaggered over to the Masters' van. Both their faces were nearly covered by huge cowboy hats. One man's hat was black and the other was made of straw. They were pushy, talkative, and asked questions. "You all chasing tornadoes?" Black Hat asked.

"Yes," Artemis answered. "Summer vacation fun for the kids."

"So this is summer fun for kids, eh?" Black Hat said with a smirk. "The closer you get to the tornado, the better. It's not a game for old men and kids. You gotta be able to run fast."

"Well, please be careful. Tornadoes are not toys to play with," Artemis cautioned.

"OK, old man," Black Hat said, as he and Straw Hat laughed and walked back to their other friends. Black Hat's rude comment and laughter was a **flagrant** rejection of Artemis' advice.

"Dad, you're not an old man!" Curie piped up angrily.

"Thanks for saying so, Curie," Artemis said. "But to him, I am. His problem is that, despite what he says, life hasn't hit him with a really big tornado. One day it will, especially if he keeps up that careless attitude!"

The guests on the *Tornado Thrills, Inc.* tour also came by to chat and offer tips for finding tornadoes. Artemis and the kids all played dumb, acting like tourists themselves. One elderly lady advised Artemis to make sure his kids were eating healthy food. While chasing tornadoes, it was all too easy to fall into a diet of greasy hamburgers and fries. A middle-aged man talked about the uncomfortable beds in the motels nowadays. Artemis politely listened and hoped the man would not ask about his career.

At last, the tourists regrouped to their van and boarded. It lumbered down the road and out of sight. The guys in red T-shirts and their *Tornado Chaser* van sped off in the opposite direction in a cloud of dust.

After what seemed like forever, the last van, the one marked *Twister Teaser*, lurched forward and slowly followed the path of *Tornado Chaser.*

"I noticed those guys in *Twister Teaser* didn't talk to anybody," Curie said to Nick.

"Do you suppose they are scientific storm chasers like us? They seem really serious."

"Let's walk over to where they were parked," Nick said. "We might learn something about them—and the other storm chasers, especially those guys in the red T-shirts."

"Good idea," Curie said. "I noticed that when people were stretching their legs and snacking, they left garbage behind."

"We didn't, did we?" Nick asked. He hated litter and litterbugs.

"No, I was careful about that," Curie said.

The kids looked around where the three other vans were parked. They noticed only the usual gum and food wrappers until Nick's eye spied something white flapping in the breeze.

"Curie, look at this!" Nick said, as he picked up a torn piece of paper. "There's writing on this paper!"

"What does it say?" Curie asked.

Nick read the letters:

"Nick!" Curie yelled. "This looks like text messaging. I think it could be a message from MisterTwister! TTYL means 'Talk to You Later.' And 'MSTRTWSTR' is short for MisterTwister."

The kids looked at each other, stunned. Out here, in the fields of Kansas, what were the chances the note could be from Dr. Brindle?

CHAPTER TEN:

A GATHERING STORM OF CLUES

As the kids walked back to the Masters' van with their new clue, Curie said, "I don't think we should tell Dad about this note just yet. I don't want to get his hopes up."

"Yeah," said Nick, "the note could just be a strange coincidence."

"Let's consider what we know so far," Curie said. "First, we tried to contact Dr. Brindle many times but couldn't reach him. He didn't call us."

"Dad said it wasn't like Dr. Brindle to be out of touch," Nick remembered. "It was not his usual behavior."

"Then, after being on the road for a while, we still didn't hear from him. Or couldn't contact him," Curie said. "Secondly, there was that strange e-mail saying Dr. Brindle went on his own storm chasing trip and not to worry about him. He also said he doesn't have the code ready for Dad's testing. He needs to do his own testing first."

"Yeah," said Nick, "and that strange e-mail wasn't written in the way he usually writes to us. It wasn't funny or full of text messaging codes!"

"What if someone else forced him to write that e-mail?" Curie asked. "To make us think he was just not working with Dad, and to keep us from focusing on the missing Dr. Brindle—so we wouldn't worry."

"Or contact the police," Nick added.

Curie continued, as if she was thinking out loud. "Suppose he really is on a storm chasing trip like the note said. He could be with any of those people we've seen so far. Or someone else we don't know about."

"Yeah," Nick agreed. "That note could have been dropped from another van we didn't see. It was awfully dark out there for a long time. We couldn't see much of anything."

"But the note wasn't really wet, sun-bleached, or wind-torn," Curie observed. "That means it wasn't sitting on the ground for a long time. It had to be dropped just before the vans left!" Curie rubbed her forehead as she thought. "It could also mean that Dr. Brindle is in serious danger," she added. "If he dropped this note from one of those vans, it means he must have been in one of the vans. Why didn't he just get out of his van and come see us?"

"Maybe he can't get out," Nick said. "Maybe he's being held prisoner!"

All of a sudden, Nick remembered an e-mail he received before the trip that he thought was spam. "Curie! This reminds me of something," he said. "Before we left, I got an e-mail from a strange e-mail address so I didn't open it. The subject line only said '☹ cuz taken.' Do you think that expression could mean, "I am unhappy because I've been taken prisoner?"

"It could," Curie said. "How horrible! Poor Dr. Brindle." She was concerned for the man who had become her friend. "Let's check that e-mail again. And let's keep watching for any kind of strange e-mail or text message. "

Thinking of the guys in red T-shirts, Nick said, "We've seen a lot of strange characters running after tornadoes. Any one of them could be crazy enough to take Dr. Brindle's code, or Dr. Brindle himself!"

"As I said," Curie repeated, "Let's not say anything to Dad just yet. He has enough to worry about!"

CHAPTER ELEVEN:

TWISTS AND TURNS

The kids returned to the van. Their father was packing up the computer equipment. When he saw them, he said, "The storm chasers are gone. Maybe we can now have a little privacy. Could you kids please go dig up the sensors we planted in the fields? Here are some shovels."

"Sure, Dad. We'll need the sensor finder," Nick said.

Artemis gave Nick his handheld sensor finder. He turned it on. The monitor displayed not only the Masters' location, but the locations of the sensors buried in the field, marked by little blinking lights.

Nick and Curie walked in the direction of the sensors. In no time, they were digging up the little boxes.

As Nick bent over his work, he glanced up and noticed some movement behind a clump of trees on the distant horizon.

"Curie," Nick said, "Don't look now, but just kind of turn your head naturally. Check out those trees over there." Nick made a tiny motion with his finger to indicate the direction. "I think we still have company. Somebody might be spying on us."

"You're right, Nick," Curie said, as she stood up and straightened her back, pretending like she was stretching her cramped body.

"Which van is it, can you tell?" Nick asked, busily rooting up another sensor with a big black shovel.

"I can't tell. The trees are in the way," she said. "But we should have Dad drive in that direction, and see what happens!"

The kids returned to the van, lugging two big sacks of sensors along with the

shovels. They were soon packed and moving on. Pointing in the direction where she had seen a vehicle, Curie said, "Hey Dad, we think we saw a van behind those trees. Can we drive over there?"

"OK, you think something might be happening?" Artemis asked, knowing Curie's instinct for mystery-solving.

"I think somebody is tracking us, as well as a tornado!" Curie exclaimed. "They might be listening to our sensors, too."

As Artemis drove in the direction Curie suggested, they noticed a vehicle far ahead suddenly speed off and disappear around a bend in the road.

"Let's stop where they stopped," Nick suggested.

Artemis halted the van. Nick and Curie jumped out to inspect the ground.

"Curie, I think I see something over there!" Nick said, pointing to some shrubbery.

The kids scurried over to the plants. Wedged between two shrubs was a small, black, metal box.

"Curie, it's a sound sensing device," Nick said, as he picked up the box, "just like the ones we put in the ground."

"Well," Curie said, "now we know for sure somebody else is tracking tornadoes the way we are! The time has come when we have to tell Dad what's happening."

"But we don't know who used this sensor," said Nick. "We didn't get close enough to the vehicle to clearly identify it. Maybe it could be a scientist interested in chasing tornadoes."

Artemis saw Nick carrying the sensor box. He said, "Nick, bring that here. I want to see if it's one of ours!"

Nick carefully handed the box over to his father.

"It sure looks the same from the outside," Artemis said, as he turned it over in his hands. He dug in his toolbox for a screwdriver and removed the bolts to open it up. The inside mechanism was also exactly the same!

"This *is* one of ours," Artemis said, shaking his head. "Dr. Brindle designed this and had it specially made for this project."

Artemis' face suddenly turned red. He rubbed his forehead. The kids could tell their father was alarmed.

"How did this happen?" Artemis asked the kids. "Is Radnor running his own show? Has he invented something new and he's not telling me? I am totally mystified! Not to mention angry!"

"At this stage, I don't believe Dr. Brindle would run off and do his own work without involving you, Dad," Curie reasoned. "There are too many weird things going on that are just not like Dr. Brindle! You said so yourself."

The kids looked at each other. It was time to tell their father about all the clues and their thoughts.

"Dad," Curie said, "We think Dr. Brindle was kidnapped for his code. We think he was back there in one of those vans. Here, look at a note we found."

Nick showed his father the note with the text messaging TTYL–MSTRTWSTR. Curie explained the real meaning of the note and told Artemis about the first e-mail that Nick received with the subject line "☹ cuz taken."

"We think it means, 'I am sad because I was taken prisoner or hostage,'" Nick explained.

"What!" Artemis cried, his spiky hair now actually seeming to stand straight up, registering his shock. His glasses popped off his nose. "I hope this kind of talk is only a product of your vivid imaginations. But somehow, I don't think so!"

Artemis thought about it for a moment and added, "Curie, you have a great mind for solving puzzles. It's clear that you have thought this through very carefully. And Nick, you have great ideas. You kids were not named after the famous scientists Marie Curie and Nicolaus Copernicus for nothing! We have to be careful. We need more clues before we start calling the police. Now, where did my glasses go?"

Curie and Nick beamed with satisfaction, glad that their father valued their thinking abilities. Curie picked up her father's glasses and handed them to Artemis. She then wagged her finger at Nick. "Don't forget," she said, "we need to check every e-mail and text message very carefully."

The Masters returned to the motel. Only the *Tornado Thrills Inc.* van was there. The other two vans were long gone. When Artemis inquired if the other two parties in the *Twister Teaser* and *Tornado Chaser* vans had checked out, the motel manager said they had left earlier in the morning. *Where did they go?*

CHAPTER TWELVE:

TWISTS OF TEXTING

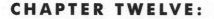

Back in their motel room, Nick peeked out the window to look at the *Tornado Thrills Inc.* van. Some of its occupants were talking in the parking lot. Nick suddenly blurted out, "Curie, I don't think anyone in that tourist group could have kidnapped Dr. Brindle!"

"I don't think so, either," Curie replied. "There would be no privacy in that van. There are just too many different types of tourists in that group—old ladies, kids, you name it."

"And Dr. Brindle is too big to be stuffed into a suitcase, or even a trunk," Nick added.

"Unless there is still another vehicle we don't know about, Dr. Brindle has to be in either *Twister Teaser* or *Tornado Chaser*," Curie said firmly.

"Who knows where those vans are now," observed Nick.

The kids powered up their laptops. "Hey, Nick," said Curie, "look up that old e-mail with the subject line '☺ cuz taken.'"

"Here it is," Nick replied. "Hey, it's an empty e-mail. It doesn't have content, just the subject line."

"Oh rats! Who's it from?" Curie asked. "Maybe that will be a clue."

"It's from 030368brain@yahoo.com," Nick said. "I have an idea; maybe those numbers stand for a special date, like a birthday."

"Dad, when is Dr. Brindle's birthday?" Curie asked.

"I think it's in March sometime, early March," Artemis replied.

"This could be Dr. Brindle's birthday— 030368 could mean March 3, 1968," Curie told the others. "So this could be his message."

"Dr. Brindle did tell me he was born in 1968," Artemis commented. "You kids amaze me!"

Curie sorted through her text messages. Her friends wanted to know how her trip was going. They often made up creative abbreviations, each person trying to outdo the other in shortening the words. "Just wondering how you are?" easily became "j/w how r u?"

Curie noticed one odd message. "This one is really strange," she said. "I know text messaging has some odd twists, but, boy, whoever sent this is really stretching things. I can't read it, and I'm an expert. It's a strange sequence of letters and periods—almost like a programming language. It's signed Rgent."

"I'll bet that means 'Urgent!'" Nick said, sitting up in his seat in anticipation.

"Read it!" Artemis yelled, as he sat down at his laptop computer, his glasses on a chain clattering as they hit the desktop. Curie started to read the sequence of letters. Hearing the familiar text he had once tried to write himself, her father shouted, "That's it! It's that short line of code I need! Radnor Brindle somehow got it to us! Curie, please send it to me."

Curie quickly forwarded the text message to her father.

"Dad," Nick said cautiously, "don't forget to save the code to the program after you get it." Artemis was so excited that his hair was sticking straight up again. Nick was sure he would forget the all-important details.

"I got it!" Artemis shouted. "What's he up to, sending the code to Curie this way? Why didn't he send it to me in regular e-mail?"

"Dad, I think this is one more clue that tells us he can't send messages the usual way," Curie replied, trying to calm Artemis. "Maybe he's a prisoner."

"Wait a minute," Nick snapped, "we don't know if this is the real code. It could be just a **ruse**. If Dr. Brindle is a prisoner, maybe his captors forced him to send a fake code!"

"Dad," Curie asked, "is there a way you can now tell if the code is good or not—without activating the whole program?"

"Someone might be able to, but I can't," Artemis replied. "I was never that great at programming. That's why I had Dr. Brindle do this piece of code. I think we will just have to wait and run the program when there's another tornado—if we don't hear anything more from Dr. Brindle!"

"Let's try e-mailing him back at his birthday address at yahoo.com," Nick suggested. Once again, both kids tried to send e-mails and text messages all through the evening, but received no reply.

Before going to bed, Curie plopped down on the couch next to Artemis. She was very worried about Dr. Brindle. "Dad, I think you should do something to help Dr. Brindle," she said. "This situation needs explaining to the authorities."

"You are right, Curie," he said. "I should have thought of that. I've been so distracted. I will e-mail the dean at Dr. Brindle's college, tell him the situation, and ask if he has heard anything."

Artemis received a prompt reply from the dean. The dean didn't know where Dr. Brindle was. He thought Dr. Brindle was with Artemis! His office would submit a Missing Persons Report to the police.

Not able to sleep, Artemis and the kids stayed up late, listening to the latest weather reports. All forecasts promised severe thunderstorms for the next evening about 50 miles east of their motel. Could this be their big opportunity to test Dr. Brindle's code and the Tornado Early Warning Device?

Curie also wondered if there would be another opportunity to contact Dr. Radnor Brindle. She was sure he was in danger. Could they do more to help him?

CHAPTER THIRTEEN

GMTA— GREAT MINDS THINK ALIKE

The next morning, Artemis and the kids packed up the van and headed to the area where thunderstorms were predicted. Once they reached the spot, they were glad to see that no other storm chasers had the same plan. The Masters had the place to themselves. The kids unpacked the sensors, grabbed some shovels and set out to bury the black boxes along the side of the road. Once their work was done, they explored an old abandoned house close to the road.

It was just about noon. Artemis suggested they go to a little town nearby to get some lunch. About an hour later, they returned with a bag full of freshly-made chicken sandwiches, oranges, and bananas. They parked under a big shade tree where they had a good view of the sensors' locations. In the distance, they could barely see the abandoned house they had explored.

Nick was finishing off the last bite of his sandwich when he turned to see a van approaching. "Oh no," he said, "we've got company!"

Curie and Artemis turned their heads to look. It was the *Tornado Thrills Inc.* tourist bus. Everyone let out a groan.

"I hope they don't find those sensors we buried!" Nick exclaimed.

The Masters watched as the tourists got out of their van to set up a picnic lunch on the side of the road. An elderly man spread a few blankets on the ground. A big woman plopped down on a blanket with a **THUD** and handed out food to the others.

"Dad," Nick said a bit angrily, "that lady's bottom is sitting right on top of where I buried a sensor!"

"Well, if we hear weird noises...," Curie began, but couldn't continue because she was overcome with giggles.

Nick glared at his sister, "Dad, should I go ask her to move?"

"Nick, let's not do anything," Artemis said. "It's only one sensor. I'd rather these people not know what we're doing."

Artemis and the kids continued to watch the tourists from inside their van.

As predicted, the sky filled with more and more towering thunderclouds as the afternoon wore on. The menacing clouds encouraged the tourists to pack up their blankets and picnic baskets and board their bus.

"A mighty storm is brewing," Artemis said, as he prepared his equipment. This time, he remembered to secure his laptop with a seatbelt.

Nick and Curie scanned the horizon and the road ahead of them. Then they got a jolt, and it wasn't from lightning. *Tornado Chaser* was headed their way with its guys in the red T-shirts!

"Thank goodness we already buried the sensors," Nick said.

The guys in red T-shirts waved as they drove by, recognizing the Masters' van. The driver of *Tornado Chaser* found a spot to park about 30 yards behind the Masters' van. The scruffy young men got out and played a quick game of Frisbee under the darkening sky until a jagged lightning bolt sent them scampering back to their van.

Watching the scene, Nick and Curie broke up laughing. Nick said, "They might not be afraid of tornadoes, but they are sure scared of lightning!"

"That may have looked funny, Nick," said Artemis, "but they were wise to seek shelter when lightning strikes. Lightning is not to be ignored."

"I know, Dad, you're right," Nick answered. "I read that more than 1,000 people are struck by lightning each year in the United States."

"I'm glad you know that, kids," Artemis said. "Don't forget it!"

Wild, fast-moving gray clouds brought the rain, which started in small drops but got bigger and bigger. Soon, it sounded as if each drop weighed a pound as they s p la tte d on the van windshield.

The kids again scanned the horizon.

"Not again!" Nick said. "I don't believe it. *Twister Teaser* is here, too!"

"We all must be listening to the same reports," Artemis said, as he and the kids watched *Twister Teaser* pull off the road behind them.

Based on all the clues they had, Curie could not help but think that Dr. Brindle was close by and was held prisoner in the rear seat of either *Twister Teaser* or *Tornado Chaser.*

The storm was rapidly building with strong gusts of wind buffeting the sides of the van, making it rock. The awful waiting began again as everyone anxiously peered at the thunderstorm raging around them.

The disturbing clack, clack of hail added to the *whoosh*, DRIP, and *slap* of heavy rain as it pelted the van. The din became horrific.

Cure had an idea to keep her mind busy. She would try to text message Dr. Brindle. If he tried to reach her before, he would try again. That's what I would do, Curie thought. Dr. Radnor had said she thought like him. Didn't he sometimes text her *GMTA*, meaning *Great Minds Think Alike*?

If he is able, he might respond, Curie thought. It could be that the others in Dr. Brindle's van were so engrossed in the storm that they wouldn't notice him in the back seat texting a message. They would notice a phone call with voices speaking, but not the *tap, tap, tap* of key punching.

In the back seat, out of earshot from their father who was preparing his equipment, Curie whispered her plan to Nick.

"It's about time you had a good idea," Nick said, teasing his sister.

Curie pulled her cell phone out of her jeans pocket. Her fingers nimbly danced over the keys as she texted her greeting to Dr. Brindle. Then she keyed in "where r u"?

Curie and Nick could hardly believe their eyes as they watched a return message appear on the tiny cell phone screen. Curie gasped. "It's him!"

"I know what he's saying," Nick said. "*In the T/T van, rolling on the floor laughing, alive, and smiling. Great minds think alike.*"

"T/T van must mean *Twister Teaser* van," Curie reasoned. She was so excited she had to tell Artemis.

"Dad!" Curie yelled to her father up front. "I got a message from Dr. Brindle! I bet he's in the *Twister Teaser* van. To say he is alive and smiling must mean he is in some kind of danger, but is basically OK. He must be held in the van against his will, rolling on the floor!"

"And knowing him," Nick said, "he is probably laughing!"

But Curie could only wonder just how much danger their friend might be in!

CHAPTER FOURTEEN:

REAPING THE WHIRLWIND

A fierce gust of wind smacked the side of the van like a giant's punch.

"Buckle your seatbelts!" Artemis yelled to his kids, "and watch for a funnel. If you see something, I want you to tell me where it is by the face of a clock. Pretend you are in the middle of the clock where the dials turn. If the funnel is over to the left directly beside us, say it is at 9 o'clock. If it is directly behind us, say it is at 6 o'clock."

"I get it," Nick said. "If the funnel is directly in front of us, we say 12 o'clock."

"You got it, now start looking!" Artemis ordered.

"I can hardly see anything," Nick said to Curie as he buckled up. "Buckets of rain must be hitting the windshield all at once!"

Artemis added to his instructions, "And remember to listen for a loud roar."

"There's a lot of noise outside now, Dad," Nick yelled, trying to be heard above the din.

Artemis gave Curie the red warning device that used to be in the Masters' living room. "Hold this beeper. Now that we have the code from Dr. Brindle, it should beep an alarm if a tornado touches down nearby."

Curie gingerly cradled the warning device in her hands. In these conditions, holding that little red box felt like holding a time bomb!

Artemis powered up the computer. Despite the howling wind outside, the kids heard his laptop hum as it jumped to life.

"The data is coming in from the sensors you buried along the road!" Artemis shouted. "And the computer's calculating. So far, so good..."

A sudden, loud roar, like a train passing over them, shook the van.

"**Beep! Breeeep! Beep!**" screeched the little red box, making Curie jump with surprise.

"Dad!" Curie yelled. "The warning device is beeping!"

"Dad!" Nick yelled even louder, to be heard over the raucous beeping and the mighty roar. "The beeper's working! There IS a big funnel at 4 o'clock! It's dark grayish brown, moving east and away from us!"

As the beeper screeched, the kids watched the funnel swerve left and right, like a menacing, stampeding bull, sucking up everything in its path for lunch, and spewing out the leftovers.

"Wow!" Nick yelled. "Junk is flying around inside the funnel. It's heading to that old, abandoned house!"

"The house is exploding!" Curie screamed, as she watched the house disintegrate, shattering into a million tiny flying missiles. A piece of board shot out of the house, like a cannon ball hurtling toward the van windshield!

"We're out of here!" Artemis said, as he stomped on the gas pedal. "We're getting to a safer place!"

"Aw, Dad," Nick whooped, "this is REALLY exciting! Look, the *Tornado Chaser* van is heading right toward the tornado!"

"Those crazy kids!" Artemis yelled. "They will get themselves killed."

Artemis drove as quickly as he could away from the tornado.

"Dad, can't we turn this alarm off?" Curie yelled. "It's killing my ears!"

"It'll stop soon," Artemis said, as he leaned forward, trying to see the road ahead through the blanket of rain pounding on his windshield.

"We're not the only ones running away," Nick yelled to Curie. "That tourist van is driving even faster than us."

Sure enough, *Tornado Thrills Inc.* had experienced its thrill and was now high-tailing out of the area. The van passed them as if the Masters' van was standing still. Other cars dashed madly in both directions. Some were chasing the storm and some were running away from it.

The screaming wind tossed tree branches and pieces of dirt everywhere. From out of nowhere, a white-tailed deer leaped across the road in front of the Masters' van.

"Dad," Nick yelled, "watch out for the deer!"

Artemis had to swerve to miss the animal. The kids grabbed the equipment as it jostled around in the van.

"In case you haven't already," Artemis yelled, holding his chin up so his glasses wouldn't slide off his nose, "you can add driving to your list of tornado hazards!"

With blinding rain, fierce wind blowing debris all about, and so many frightened drivers and animals on the road, driving near a tornado was almost as dangerous as being caught in the tornado, Curie thought.

The blasting beeper finally shut off on its own.

"My ears!" Curie complained. "My ears are ringing! It was SO loud!"

"Good," Artemis said. "We know it'll wake people up!"

When they reached a safe distance where Artemis could stop and think clearly, Curie said, "Dad, you should call the dean or the police about that text message I got from Dr. Brindle. I am sure he's in the *Twister Teaser* van."

"Did either of you kids see what happened to that van?" Artemis asked.

Curie and Nick looked at each other. "No, we didn't notice," Curie answered. We just saw the tourist van run away, like we did, and the *Tornado Chaser* chase the tornado!"

"Now that the tornado has blown away from the area," Curie asked her dad, "can we go back there? I know we need to retrieve the sensors, but maybe we can find out what happened to *Twister Teaser.*"

Curie and Nick wondered if Twister Teaser and Tornado Chaser got too close to the tornado. If so, what had happened to Radnor Brindle?

CHAPTER FIFTEEN

GONE WITH THE WIND

Artemis sent an e-mail to the dean about the strange message from Dr. Brindle indicating he was in the *Twister Teaser* van. Then Artemis described the apparent success of the Tornado Early Warning Device. Final success couldn't be declared until the computer program was re-run and evaluated. So far, though, things looked good.

"Look, Dad," Nick said, as his father shut down the laptop, "the storm is clearing."

Artemis scanned the brightening skies. "I guess we can go get the sensors now," he said. As the van approached the general area, the devastation became more and more apparent. Tree branches and sparking power lines were strewn all over the road.

Using the binoculars, the kids could make out the 300-foot-wide path the tornado had taken across hedges, trees, fields, and fences. It was as if a giant lawn mower had cut through it all. Everything in the path was either flattened or gone!

"Look!" Curie exclaimed. "That old abandoned house isn't there anymore!"

The kids scrambled out of the van and surveyed the scene. The only thing left of the house was the cement foundation and a few pieces of board and debris.

"I don't see *Twister Teaser* or *Tornado Chaser,*" Nick said.

Curie, ever the sleuth, stood with her hands on her hips, thinking. "Let's see where *Twister Teaser* was parked and look for tire tracks. Maybe we can tell the direction they took."

The kids scanned the ground where the van was parked. Sure enough, it looked like

the van had gone in the direction of the tornado! Beyond the tire marks, there was no sign that anybody had been there.

While the kids gathered the sensors, they wondered what happened to the two vans and to Dr. Brindle.

"Dad, can you put a call in to the police," Curie pleaded. "Please just tell them we think Dr. Brindle is in the *Twister Teaser* van and may be held against his will. Don't tell them about the text messaging part."

This was a real test of Artemis' trust in his daughter's analytical abilities. "OK," Artemis said, "will do." He dialed 911 on his cell phone, asking to be connected to the police.

When Artemis and the kids returned to the motel room, the phone was ringing. Everyone looked at each other. Who was it? Artemis picked up the receiver and said, "Hello." There was a pause, and then he whooped, "Radnor! Where are you?"

The kids jumped up and down and high-fived each other. Dr. Brindle was safe!

Artemis paced the floor as he spoke with his friend, telling him everything that had happened. Finally, he hung up the phone and whirled around to face the kids.

"We are going to pick up Dr. Brindle," Artemis said, excited. "Let's go!"

When Dr. Brindle was safely checked into his room, Artemis and the kids asked him to tell his story. He said that two of his former co-workers, who were **disgruntled** because they didn't get research funding, tried to steal the code. When that didn't work, they dragged off Dr. Brindle at the last moment and kept him prisoner in the van.

"Did they make you send that odd e-mail?" Curie asked. "I didn't think it sounded like you!"

"Oh yes," Dr. Brindle said, "but not before I managed to send off that e-mail from my yahoo.com e-mail address. They nearly caught me on that one."

"We got that one!" Nick said. "We finally figured out it was from you. I nearly deleted that e-mail because I didn't recognize the sender."

Dr. Brindle turned to Curie. "My dear," he said, "your idea to call the police helped me. Also, I have you to thank for teaching me text messaging! That's what saved me. In all the tornado excitement, the bad guys couldn't hear me text message in the rear of the van. They would have heard me if I tried to make a 911 call."

"GMTA!" Curie replied. "Great Minds Think Alike. I knew you would think that way!" Curie wrapped her arms around Dr. Brindle in a bear hug.

Curie looked over at Nick. "I have to admit," she said, "my little brother here helped a lot with his bright ideas! I can't claim all the credit for solving the puzzle and finding you!"

"Aw, it was nothing," Nick said modestly, but he was pleased that his sister recognized his abilities.

"I also have to admit," Curie added, "that I never suspected those clean-cut, professional-looking guys in *Twister Teaser*. That means I still have much to learn about sleuthing and mystery solving! I was misled by a red herring!"

"We thought those grungy red T-shirt guys in *Tornado Chaser* might have kidnapped you," Nick explained. "You can't judge a book by its cover!"

Radnor asked Artemis if he had done the final test of the program to see if they had true success with the Tornado Early Warning Device.

"Let's see!" said Artemis, as he powered up his computer. The program started its last sequence with, *You have all the data for final analysis. Kick the tires and light the fires!* Everyone laughed, and Curie rolled her eyes at Dr. Brindle.

Artemis hit the command key to calculate the data. The computer hummed for a moment and then a pop-up box jumped up on the screen with the message *PROGRAM SUCCESSFUL!*

Artemis closed the pop-up and double checked the calculations. It had all worked—perfectly! Artemis thrust both of his arms into the air. "Yessssss!" he shouted, and nearly fell over backwards in his chair. Curie quickly grabbed him and planted a big kiss on his cheek.

"You did it, Dad!" Nick shouted. "So, what disaster do we tackle next?"

Everyone laughed—but no one unpacked their bags. They knew better!

THE END

ABOUT THE AUTHOR

Carole Marsh is an author and publisher who has written many works of fiction and non-fiction for young readers. She travels throughout the United States and around the world to research her books. In 1979, Carole Marsh was named Communicator of the Year for her corporate communications work with major national and international corporations.

Marsh is the founder and CEO of Gallopade International, established in 1979. Today, Gallopade International is widely recognized as a leading source of educational materials for every state and many countries. Marsh and Gallopade were recipients of the 2004 Teachers' Choice Award. Marsh has written more than 50 Carole Marsh Mysteries™. In 2007, she was named Georgia Author of the Year. Years ago, her children, Michele and Michael, were the original characters in her mystery books. Today, they continue the Carole Marsh Books tradition by working at Gallopade. By adding grandchildren Grant and Christina as new mystery characters, she has continued the tradition for a third generation.

Ms. Marsh welcomes correspondence from her readers. You can e-mail her at fanclub@gallopade.com, visit carolemarshmysteries.com, or write to her in care of Gallopade International, P.O. Box 2779, Peachtree City, Georgia, 30269 USA.

BOOK CLUB
TALK ABOUT IT!

1. Can you remember the scariest storm you've ever been in? What did you do?

2. What part of the Masters' tornado chasing adventure did you find most exciting?

3. Would you ever want to see a tornado up close? Why or why not?

4. Where is the safest place in YOUR house to go if there's a storm? Have you ever had to retreat there because of a tornado warning or other form of severe weather?

5. Why do you think *The Wizard of Oz* was set in Kansas?

6. Why do tornadoes and hurricanes rotate in different directions depending on their location on the globe?

7. If you had a van to chase storms in, what would you call it?

8. What parts of the story made you laugh?

BOOK CLUB
BRING IT TO LIFE!

1. Dr. Brindle communicated with the Masters kids through the trendy, cryptic method of text message lingo. Exchange notes with a friend using abbreviations and emoticons and see who can decode their note first!

2. Nick and Curie were very specific about the importance of a well-stocked safe room in case of a tornado. Gather items mentioned in the book and create a Tornado Warning Safety Box.

3. Draw a map of the United States. Label the states. With a bold marker, draw a line through Tornado Alley. Where do you live in relation to this line?

4. Designate a place in the classroom as a mock safe room. Set a timer for five minutes and walk around the room, talk with your friends, work on a project, etc. When the timer goes off, stage a practice tornado drill and quickly get to the part of the room that is the safe room. Make sure to take time to pretend to turn off the electricity and gas. Once everyone is in the safe zone and properly ducked and covered, check to see how much time it took to get there safely. Can you do all of that in 15 seconds like the Masters kids?

TORNADO SCAVENGER HUNT

Go on a Scavenger Hunt around your classroom and/or school for these 10 items to create a Tornado Safety Box for your class. Remember to ask before taking any items for the box!

1. —— Flashlight

2. —— Cell phone

3. —— Batteries

4. —— Bottled water

5. —— Band Aids

6. —— Battery-powered radio

7. —— Canned foods

8. —— Can opener

9. —— Clothes

10. —— Swiss army knife

TORNADO POP QUIZ

1. Where is the best place to go in a house if there's a tornado warning?

2. What were the names of the three vans in the story?

3. How many different states did the Masters visit on their tornado chase?

4. Why didn't Curie like being so close to Nick during their tornado drill?

5. Why didn't Dr. Brindle respond to phone calls from Nick, Curie, and Artemis?

6. What did the numbers in Dr. Brindle's e-mail address mean?

7. What is the difference between a tornado watch and a tornado warning?

8. What are some important signs in the weather that a tornado is nearby or forming?

GLOSSARY

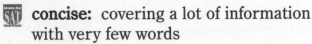

 antagonism: hostility or opposition

 concise: covering a lot of information with very few words

debris: that which is left over after something has been destroyed

din: a loud, continuous noise

 disgruntled: displeased and discontented

disintegrate: to break up

flagrant: very noticeable or obvious

red herring: a misleading clue meant to take away attention from the actual problem

 ruse: a trick

GLOSSARY

seismic: having to do with a shaking of the earth

sleuth: a detective

vortex: a whirling mass of water, air, or fire that is visible in the form of a column, funnel, or spiral

TORNADO TRIVIA

1. A tornado can toss a 2000-to-3000-pound van into the air!

2. A tornado that forms over water is known as a "waterspout."

3. The strongest tornadoes can last for over an hour!

4. In April of 1991, the Plains states saw 54 tornadoes in one day!

5. Tornadoes can happen at any time, but they are most likely to form between 3 p.m. and 9 p.m.

TORNADO TRIVIA

6. In the most extreme cases, a tornado's winds can reach up to 300 miles per hour.

7. Tornadoes may not be visible until after the funnel has picked up debris.

8. The destruction from a tornado can cover a very long path. In 1953, chunks of a mattress from Worcester, Massachusetts ended up in Boston Harbor, 50 miles away!

9. Generally speaking, most tornadoes travel from southwest to northeast.

10. Tornadoes have been described as sounding like a train, a jet plane, or a waterfall.

TECH CONNECTS

Hey, Kids!
Visit www.carolemarshmysteries.com to:

Join the Carole Marsh Mysteries Fan Club!

Write one sensational sentence using all five
SAT words in the glossary!

Download a Tornado Word Search!

Take a Pop Quiz!

Download a Scavenger Hunt!

Get Treacherous Tornado Trivia!

Read Tornado Safety Tips!